P9-DMT-281

THE
BIG NIGHT
Out

Thor Wickstrom

Dial Books for Young Readers New York

Published by Dial Books for Young Readers
A Division of Penguin Books USA Inc.
375 Hudson Street
New York, New York 10014

Library of Congress Cataloging in Publication Data
Wickstrom, Thor.
The big night out / by Thor Wickstrom.—1st ed.
p. cm.
Summary: Bear, Mouse, and Goose go out for a night on the town.
ISBN 0-8037-1170-0.—ISBN 0-8037-1171-9 (lib. bdg.)
[1. Bears—Fiction. 2. Moose—Fiction. 3. Geese—Fiction.]
I. Title.
PZ7.W6296Bi 1993 [E]—dc20 91-46563 CIP AC

The full-color artwork was prepared using pen and ink, watercolor,
and gouache. It was then scanner-separated and reproduced as red,
blue, yellow, and black halftones.

For my dad, the original Bear

The mouse and the goose and the grizzly bear
Went out for a night on the town.

They hopped in a cab
(At the wheel was a crab)
And they rode to a nightclub uptown.
Bump! Bump! Bump!
They rode to a nightclub uptown!

The mouse was dressed up in a fine checkered suit,
The goose wore a tall crimson hat.
The bear wore a cape he had sewn from a drape,
With a monocle and a cravat.
(What a dude!)
With a monocle and a cravat!

They gave the crab-driver a generous tip,

And swaggered on into the club.

The mouse and the goose
Drank a tumbler of juice,
While the bear ate a barrel of grub
At the bar.
While the bear ate a barrel of grub!

The dance band was playing a rip-roaring tune,
The bear and a fox took the floor.
The mouse with a cat
And the goose with a rat

Were calling and bawling for more,
One more time!
Were calling and bawling for more!

They danced and they pranced till a quarter to six,

They roared and they squeaked and they honked!

But on reaching the street
They looked haggard and beat,
"Gadzooks, I feel totally zonked!"
Said the bear.
"Gadzooks, I feel totally zonked!"

"That was fun," said the goose.
"Now let's hop in a cab
  And ride home the same way we came!"
"I'm afraid," said the mouse,
"We must walk to our house,
  For we haven't a cent to our name.
  What a shame!
  For we haven't a cent to our name!"

"Don't despair!" said the bear
  to his two tired friends.
"Now you guys just listen to me!
I know this old goat,
And he paddles a boat,
We might all get a ride home for free.
Yessiree.
We might all get a ride home for free."

But to reach the goat's dock, our friends had to walk
Eighty blocks on their poor tired feet.

They should have thought twice—
Taken Mouse's advice—
It was forty blocks back to the street
Where they lived,
Just forty blocks back to their street!

They found Mister Goat sitting out on his boat,
And Bear told of their night on the town.

"...So you see, we are broke,
Now I beg of you, Goat,
Could you pretty-please paddle us down,
Back downtown?
Could you pretty-please paddle us down?"

"Your story is sad," said the goat with a grin. "You are all tuckered out, and it shows!

But I don't work for free,
So to ride back with *me,*
You must pay me with all of your clothes—
Hats and all!
You must pay me with all of your clothes!"

The mouse gave his clothes to that greedy old goat,
The goose gave his coat and his hat.

And to cover *his* fare,
That embarrassed old bear,
Gave his monocle, cape, and cravat
To the goat!
Gave his monocle, cape, and cravat!

So Goat paddled off with our three blushing friends,
Who were naked as naked could be.
And from Mr. Goat's dock
One and all came to gawk,

At Goat and his bare crew of three!
Hee! Hee! Hee!
At Goat and his bare crew of three!

Though they heard the crowd roar,
As they rowed from the shore,
Those three naked friends didn't laugh.

And when Bear, Goose, and Mouse
Finally got to their house,

They slept for a day and a half!
They were beat!
They slept for a day and a half!